THE GHOSTS *of* YEARNING

THE GHOSTS *of* YEARNING

A Gothic Short Story About Profound Loss and

the Boundaries of the Real and the Unreal

GEORGE G. KITCHENS III

Photo credits to:
Author Photo by: Amanda Jo Brown
Cover Model: Mick Alan Ricci and Photo courtesy of Kaitlyn Greenly

Library of Congress Control Number: 2017903999
ISBN: Hardcover   978-1-5245-9222-6
                   Softcover   978-1-5245-9221-9
                   eBook   978-1-5245-9220-2

Print information available on the last page.

Rev. date: 03/17/2017

To order additional copies of this book, contact:
Xlibris
1-888-795-4274
www.Xlibris.com
Orders@Xlibris.com
756978

Contents

How the handsome and charismatic David Blank
impacts the lives of three haunted women

George G. Kitchens III

For Stephen:

Love is never a burden

We yearn for what once was

We yearn to keep what is now

We yearn for things that never were

————●————

1

Gliding

GLIDING AS THOUGH a ghost.

That's the best way to describe Maisie Dearborn as she pushed her walker through the halls of the facility. It could be called gliding because she used her walker in such a way that it looked like she and it were hovering slightly above the floor as she made her way down the hall. Peering over a desktop counter, one could see her pass by in an almost fluid motion with only an occasional bob in her movement. As adept and skillful as she was while navigating her walker through the halls of E-wing for all the long years she had lived at the facility, she couldn't walk a single step without it.

David Blank, the director of this wing of the facility, a large medical compound that included a hospital, a comprehensive extended care wing, retirement village, and a research campus, was ready to leave for the evening. He dedicated himself to making rounds every day through each of the sections he supervised. As usual at this time of the day, he passed by Maisie Dearborn gliding down the long corridor of E-wing, the section that specialized in long-term comprehensive patient care. Elderly and infirm as she was, Miss Maisie, for everyone called Maisie Dearborn "Miss Maisie," was nevertheless likewise dedicated to her daily rituals, including this exercise. His last few steps approaching her were done in a mocked speeding-up fashion.

"Good evening, Miss Maisie," David said as she stopped her forward progress for just a moment to give him a once-over with her old eyes. David was a tall and strikingly handsome man with chiseled features and a natural charm that quickly won over anyone with whom he came into contact. A genuinely incorruptible man, just a brief exchange with David made one feel as though they had just experienced a satisfyingly transcendent encounter. So who could blame an old woman, well past her eighties and possibly in her nineties, for stopping to experience the same gratifying once-over glances that many much younger women, and more than a few men, would give?

"On your way home, David?"

"You know I am, Miss Maisie. And you know what else? I time the end of my day to coincide with your early evening walks, just so I can see if I can still keep up with you. And it appears as though some days I *almost* can." Actually, Maisie timed her evening walks to coincide with David's last rounds. She loved structure and organization in the small confined world in which she now existed. And she certainly enjoyed the platonic flirtation and attention from such a handsome young man.

"Don't forget to take the garbage out tonight, David." So structured was she and so sharp her mind that she even remembered which routines went with which days of the week of those around her. She hadn't forgotten that David once told her about how he had neglected to put the garbage out one week and had gotten "quite the scolding" from his wife. It was during the heat of summer, and it would be another long week for whatever was in the trash at the time to sit around and fester in the car garage.

David chuckled, "Ahhh yes, Miss Maisie, Wednesday night. Garbage night. Thanks for the reminder. I'm sure I will get another one at home." Actually, the long-ago incident had passed beyond everyday memory, and his wife wouldn't even think to remind him. But for David and Maisie, this was a weekly ritual. Structured. Organized. Comforting.

Maisie continued to glide through the length of the corridor, at the end of which was a stairwell. The stairwell door was labeled with a plaque numbered 121 on it. Even though it wasn't a room, state code and fire regulations mandated that all doors in facilities such as these be labeled with a number to aid in locating specific areas during emergencies. The door led outside for this was the first floor, and the stairwell also led upstairs to the next two levels of the three-story building. The end of the corridor had a large window that looked out onto a small adjacent wooded area outside of that wing, but she never went that far. It was the door before the stairwell door, the one labeled 119, that marked Maisie's destination and turning point. This door, and the paintings bookending it, she gazed at for several minutes each day as she took a brief rest. This was as far as she could make it in order to turn around and get back to her own room without exhausting herself, thus perpetuating the perception that she made her daily strolls so effortlessly.

On her swing back down the hall, close to the large nursing desk where three sections of hallway met to form a T, she passed Old Man Perkinson, who often sat in the corridor that was her daily route. Now the reason he got the moniker "Old Man Perkinson" is because he was just as cantankerous as an old man as Maisie was a sweet and loveable little old lady. He was the quintessentially crotchety old man.

"Hello again, Arthur."

"You just said hello a few minutes ago when you whizzed by me the first time."

"That's why I said 'hello again', Arthur," said Maisie with a little chuckle and barely a note of reprimand in her voice. "Looks like a beautiful day outside."

"I'm not in the mood for small talk." The crankiness effortlessly flowed out of Arthur Perkinson. "My pacemaker isn't working again today. I can feel my arrhythmia, and it's not doing a dang thing to correct it. And they made me sit here just so I can watch you racing up and down the halls, and I know they do it 'cause they think I need exercise too. And I'm not in the mood to race." In reality, "they" didn't make him do anything. He was a man of rituals much like Maisie was a woman with her own. Rituals that must be adhered to, rituals that ward off the inevitable that is often forefront in the minds of those who spend their "golden years" in well-intentioned confinement.

Miss Maisie took yet another break, this time to sit down beside Old Man Perkinson, and again he said, "I told you I'm not in the mood for small talk." But small talk they did. It wasn't a romance, but anyone who viewed the spectacle of the cantankerous old man and the loveable old woman would've thought that their spatting and sparring resembled an old couple who'd been together for decades.

David finished his rounds by stopping at the nearby main nurse's desk of E-wing to bid everyone a good evening, signaling that all was in order. Victoria Quinones-Soto, the secretary at the desk, signaled back and gave him a long glance, one slightly more lustful in nature than the one Miss Maisie had given as she watched him go on his way.

Everyone else in the vicinity of the station was too entrenched in their work to do more than either good-naturedly grunt a good-bye or give a quick hand wave. Simone, a nurse working on the computer, didn't turn around, but her backward hand wave caused a few of the beads at the end of the long, black braids that ran down her back to hit each other, making a light clanking sound to show that at least she was acknowledging his departure. Dr. Ekema Olinga, a generally well-mannered hospitalist who hailed from Cameroon, stationed at another computer, also kept his back to the others and either didn't hear the "good-byes" or was just too preoccupied to acknowledge anything while studying his patients' charts. Tiffany, a bubbly young nurse, just kept on babbling to anyone who would listen to her babble, her big poof of highlighted hair bouncing on her head as she moved. Just a group of people who were all going through their daily routines while David finished his and two elderly people sat nearby performing their own set of rituals. The routines and rituals of work life, of life itself.

Maisie eventually returned to her room.

David left the building and drove home.

2

Sandwiches

THE REFRIGERATOR IN the ranch-style house was cluttered with various magnets and clippings, coupons and notes. It was the one area of the kitchen that was not spotless and tidy. Everything else was neat and orderly. Everything was in its place. But the refrigerator was a refuge from all the orderliness. One rather large partially folded newspaper clipping on the side of the unit was so old and worn that it should've been better preserved or else discarded years ago, but as it had sentimental value, it was only ever moved from its spot once, when the refrigerator itself was replaced.

Amid a faint greenish-gray glow that came from another room in the house, Helen McCardle stood at the kitchen counter next to the refrigerator preparing two sandwiches. Perfectly prepared, perfectly sliced, with the perfect ingredients. Helen was not a perfectionist or at least she didn't think so. But she was accustomed to certain things, and as long as certain things were so, they could not change. And most change was not good. She wasn't too old for change; she just detested it. A seemingly vibrant woman of sixty-seven, Helen McCardle had very few cracks that permeated her stoic exterior. Long retired due to good investments, shrewd financial planning, and meticulous money management, Helen had everything perfectly planned, and simply chose it to be this way. The perfect one-story house built over forty-one years ago, the perfect cleanliness and order of her home, the perfectly cut sandwiches she made on the counter. It was a lot of exhausting work to maintain this home that stood on the outskirts of town, several miles removed from the medical facility, all by herself, but Helen cherished her home and was determined that this is how her life would stay.

He sat wordlessly in a big, comfy chair in the room that adjoined the kitchen, the room which created the faint glow. A classically handsome and much younger man than Helen, he was pale in visage, with an otherworldly luminescence about him. In fact, the greenish-gray glow emanated directly from him and got slightly stronger as this glow reached other portions of the house that had visible eyesight to his presence. So pale was he that when Helen brought the sandwiches into the room, she thought that she could almost see right through him.

This room was barely distinguishable as a separate room as the wall that divided the kitchen and it had a large eight-foot archway, the result of remodeling done to the house some years ago that made the smallish home seem more open and inviting. The television was turned on to a very low volume, and the handsome pale young man mostly stared directly and completely silently at it. Helen set up two tray tables, one for him and one for her, from the broom closet and placed napkins and the small paisley-decorated lunch plates with the sandwiches on them onto the tables. Then she sat down in the smaller chair next to him.

The television was perfectly situated in front of them. Other than an occasional furtive glance and smile directed at Helen, the handsome pale young man made no moves whatsoever, no sound whatsoever, and his eyes remained fixated on the television. Helen suddenly realized that although the television had been turned on, there was nothing but snow on the screen. She noticed how he was transfixed by the static nothingness on display. His face seemed to be frozen with a faint smile as he stared at it, the greenish glow from him melding with the gray glow from the television screen created an otherworldly combination.

Helen took a few bites of her meal and looked in despair at the untouched sandwich in front of him. She looked at him. She looked over at the static snow on the television screen. She again looked over in his direction.

That damn tube. It's the only thing they meaningfully share. It was a brief but common thought that passed through her mind. It made her feel lonely, so incredibly lonely.

A few minutes later, with the handsome pale young man still glowing and unchanged in any way, and with his sandwich untouched in its entirety, Helen put the tray tables away, tidied up the area, and took the plates out to the kitchen.

Helen brushed one fully uneaten sandwich from one of the plates into the garbage.

3

Only David Will Do

MONA JEFFRIES STOOD anxiously by the window, peering out through the lace curtains at the house across the street. It would be any minute now. David would be home.

Mona and her husband Charles lived on Woods Drive on the opposite end of town in the other direction from the facility. Woods Drive was so named because it was a long stretch of road with homes on one side and mostly untouched woods along the other side. The residents had long fought to keep the area undeveloped, and had banded together to purchase the areas of the pristine woods, full of wildlife and beautifully unkempt flora, that had not already been protected by the city's clean and green program. Mona's house was one of the few on the other side of the long road, built on a patch of land that had been basically barren and designated as suitable to "steal" from nature. It also helped that she and her husband built it long ago before green initiatives had been either trendy or necessary.

Mona's husband, Charles, sat reading the daily news, alternately reading from over, under, and through his big thick-rimmed black glasses. He occasionally turned to glance through these big thick-rimmed black glasses at Mona, who stood stalkerishly at the window, and shook his head in disapproval. Charles was a dark-skinned African American with a big muscular frame and slightly graying, shortly cropped hair. His marriage to Mona had been mostly a happy and contented one. As a biracial couple, they had been blessed with wonderfully nonjudgmental family, friends, and neighbors and had lived a life that was mostly free of the racism and prejudices that are often directed at biracial marriages.

But Mona's increased fixation with this very handsome young neighbor vexed and worried him. He seldom said anything about his concerns regarding this to her as he hoped that if this is what she needed to maintain what had become an increasingly tenuous grip on sanity, then he was willing to accept it. "Why don't you leave that poor boy alone, Mona?" asked Charles in his booming baritone voice as he looked again over at her through his big thick-rimmed black glasses for the fifth time.

"Charlie, I'm not bothering David at all. He's always so nice and so willing to help. And you know that . . . only David will do," Mona said with an air of mystery and deluded whimsy in her voice.

And so she watched and waited for far more than the mere minutes she was certain it would be. Finally, she saw David Blank's car pull into his driveway and watched as the garage doors opened, and he drove his car into the wide garage. When David got out of his car, he put his briefcase on a nearby bench and immediately walked to the left side of the garage and picked up one of two garbage cans and carried it out to the edge of the driveway. It was then that Mona darted out of her house, strands of her blonde hair flailing in the wind. Her shawl flapped slightly from both her quick movement and the light wind in the air.

"David!" Mona called out to him, and he immediately looked over her way. Within a second, he forced a smile, because David was too kindhearted not to, and waved and headed back to the garage for the second garbage can. The second can was green with a large recycling decal on it, and he sat it next to the other one. By this time, Mona had reached his driveway, and so he stood and talked to her before he had even gone inside to see his own family.

He knew what was coming, for it often happened on Wednesdays, the day he would come home and put out the trash: Mona would come outside to greet him. So after a very brief exchange, it happened.

"David, I was wondering if you could stop over for just a minute . . . just a minute, David, and . . . talk to her. It would mean so much to me, and I think it would help her. You're the only one who seems to be able to make a difference," said Mona, stammering and completely unconvincingly.

David hesitated for a moment, turned, and looked briefly at his own home. But he saw the look on Mona's face. How she looked so desperate as if her whole sanity depended on his answer. And so he couldn't say no. Besides, he knew that this ritual would only take a few minutes. And much like Mona's husband, albeit on a much smaller scale, David acquiesced to what he thought would be best in the situation.

When Mona and David walked into the house, Charles, still seated with his newspaper, looked over at David through his big thick-rimmed black glasses with an exasperated look that said both "I'm sorry" and "why do you humor her this way". He again shook his head.

"Hey, Chuck, anything good in the news? I haven't had a chance yet to catch up. Mona here caught me just as I got home", David said, making sure to disarm the husband of the woman who had just strong-armed and emotionally-guilt another man to come into her husband's home.

"Same old same old, David. Stocks are down, crime is up, every celebrity is crazy, and my team got beat again". After a pause, Charles gave a slight nod in Mona's direction. "Sorry about . . . you know," he said, his booming baritone voice trailing off.

"It's no problem, really," David chuckled awkwardly, these "visits" being the only times in his life, his natural charm and ease of presence failed him. Eager to get this over with, he turned to Mona and said, "Well, shall we?"

"Oh, yes," said Mona as she led David up the nearby staircase. She then led him to a closed door, halfway down the hall on the same side that faced his house. "David," said Mona with an imperative tone in her voice, "this has been a very bad day for her, she merely needs just to see you, hear your voice. You have such a way with words, what with your background in counseling, you have such a calming effect, and it would help me relax knowing that at least something is helping her. It will only take a minute, like always, David."

She opened the door, and a faint greenish-gray glow emanated into the hallway from the otherwise darkened room. David walked in.

4

Sex on E-Wing

ARTHUR PERKINSON AND Maisie Dearborn sat in the little row of comfy chairs that was near the nursing station of E-wing, the long-term care portion of the facility where they lived. This was, of course, after Maisie's daily stroll to the other end of the corridor. Although Maisie herself never had visitors, and Arthur's visitors came only three times a year, various family members or friends would occasionally visit the other residents around this time of day. Family members who hadn't forgotten that they existed, and whatever friends were left who were still independently mobile to be able to visit "just some old folks" in an old folks' home. But mostly what Old Man Perkinson and Miss Maisie saw were strangers, kind strangers, somewhat familiar over time, who were visiting others who were also merely just some old folks in an old folks' home.

Today, it was Old Man Perkinson's hearing aid that wasn't working properly, and his frustration showed by his voice being louder than usual. Maisie shushed him a little bit and was trying to help him calm down by tenderly brushing her hand against his when a blonde-haired woman in her thirties walked by. Obviously here to visit someone else, the woman was accompanied by two elementary school-aged children. She glanced over at the couple and put her hand on her cheek, smiling with a look that read "I can't believe how sweet and heartwarming this old couple is."

"WE'RE NOT HAVING SEX!" Arthur bellowed at the woman, which raised eyebrows and widened the eyes of all those in the vicinity of his louder-than-usual voice. The staff was long accustomed to such outbursts from the cantankerous old man, and the woman with the children was not the type to act as if she were offended. She did not shield her kids' ears from such course language, but she was nonetheless a bit alarmed by the outburst and kept walking. The children just giggled as children do when someone says a naughty word, but Maisie could've sworn that she heard the little boy ask his mother "what is sex" as they continued walking down the corridor of E-wing.

"Arthur! Was that really necessary?" scolded Maisie. "I tell you she was just looking at us, two old people sitting here, who lived a long life and ended up in this place, and it looked to her like we found love again or something special in our old age to make our golden years worth living. Or maybe she thought we've been married for seventy years, who knows."

"You thought all that? You have quite an imagination if you thought all that. I'm telling you she thinks I'm boning you." All of this was said with louder than usual decibels due to his allegedly malfunctioning hearing aid.

"Arthur!"

David was making his last rounds at the nurses' desk in the near distance, and it was obvious that some discussion at the desk between Tiffany, the bouncy-haired nurse, and Victoria Quinones-Soto, the unit secretary, varied between chuckling at the cantankerous old man's outburst and debating whether it was time for his medication.

"Arthur," started Maisie as she glanced over David and the nurses at the desk, "it's you who has the overactive imagination if you think that between you with your hearing aid, your pacemaker, your joint replacements, and your cane, not to mention all your other ailments, and me with my walker and can't walk a step without it, that you think the first thing she thought was that we're having a torrid affair right here in this love palace." They both laughed so hard they had to cough. Arthur couldn't help noticing that Maisie, through her laughter, was also keeping an eye on David.

"It's a damn shame that daughter of your'n doesn't come see you," said Arthur loudly, thinking of the woman who had just passed by, the woman who was the daughter or granddaughter of someone who lived here and cared enough to visit. He had suddenly changed the subject, and it was evidence that his cranky nature can be tempered by genuine caring. But it was also changing the subject to something Maisie clearly didn't want to address. Arthur could tell she had kept her eyes in the general direction of the handsome and charismatic supervisor who was about to walk out the door in the distance.

"I suppose you'd like to turn this into a love palace with that one," said he.

"Arthur!" was again the exasperated response from the blushing senior, eager to conceal or discount any kind of untoward interest in David. "Stop talking like that," was her reply, but really, most every day, Maisie Dearborn and Arthur Perkinson shared these kinds of exchanges.

Records in the facility could pinpoint how long the two had been residents there at the same time, but to them and everyone else, it just seemed as though they had *always* existed in this manner, a friendship not attached to the confines of time.

5

A Brief Interlude

HELEN MCCARDLE EXHALED with fatigue. The puff of her breath ruffled the bangs of her slightly disheveled hair. She stood at the counter in her kitchen preparing a small meal of bologna sandwiches. The area where she prepared this meal was a bit messier than it usually was. She had mowed the lawn earlier today, and so she didn't have the energy to also clean the kitchen. Mowing the lawn in itself is not exhausting work, but lately, Helen felt more and more physical wear and tear from the daily routines and chores of keeping a house up by herself. It's not even her age so much as sixty-seven is still quite young enough to do a lot of work and not be too exhausted.

She looked over at the large newspaper clipping on the refrigerator. The old, yellowed piece of paper featured a somewhat large picture of a very handsome younger man. It was the very same handsome face with the same gentle smile as that of the handsome pale young man in the adjoining room. The date on the clipping indicated that the man in the photo would be about the same age as Helen was at the time the article ran. She turned to look toward the greenish-gray glow that came from the other room and took a deep breath that turned into a sigh. She then looked at the picture again and wept. But no, she could not weep, and so she put a stop to that immediately.

She needed to be strong. She had so much work to do; there were some minor household repairs to be done, but at least the lawn was mowed for another week. She had considered letting one of the neighbor boys mow the lawn, but at the same time, she didn't like to relinquish any control over her own life. She was determined to be strong and hold on to it as long as she could. Besides, it wasn't the lawn that exhausted her.

It was that greenish-gray glow brought such a profound fatigue.

Still, Helen finished making the sandwiches and set up the tray tables as she always did. She turned on the television and sat eating while the handsome pale young man just sat there, glowing and smiling as always. He didn't eat a single bite as always. And so his sandwich went into the trash again. Like before. Like always.

Feeling sadly resigned about having had to again eat alone, Helen turned to look at the silent man.

He was noticeably much paler today and seemed even more transparent than before. Even worse, she could've sworn he sneered at her.

Sneered! But why?

Helen couldn't take the sinister look on his face and stumbled, with only the counter and a quick firm grip with her hands to keep her from falling down. She allowed herself to weep but again for only a moment. She must be strong. She must be strong.

On the other side of town, Mona walked up the stairs to the room she had previously taken David to. As she opened the door, the faint greenish-gray glow filtered from the otherwise darkened room. She very slowly walked over to the window and pulled at the blinds, looking forlornly across the street. It looked like a cold gray day outside, made even colder by the silence and still appearance of the house across the street.

"David won't be able to come over today," said Mona dejectedly as she stood looking through the blinds, lightly caressing the length of each wooden slat that was at breast level. "He's away on vacation. I'm so sorry. I know how much his little visits mean to you, no matter how brief they are. How they're helping you to get stronger. How one day you will be all better and be able to leave this room. And be whole again after all that has happened."

The greenish-gray glow in the room was faint but constant behind her.

Mona's words met with silence. And she didn't even bother to turn around at all while she spoke.

At the facility, located in a third area of town, equidistant from the other two, there was a continuation of life at the place of the nearing of the end-of-life. David wasn't on E-wing today, his duties having been expanded to include other sections of the large medical facility due to a major promotion; in fact, it was now rare to see David in this portion of the facility at all. In the large nurses' station in the middle of the long corridor, Simone, Dr. Olinga, Tiffany, and the rest of the staff went about the duties their careers brought them here to do. But the secretary, Victoria Quinones-Soto, was preoccupied, distracted once again by the marvel of seemingly impossible mechanics. She couldn't help but stare at the sight in front of her.

Miss Maisie was effortlessly gliding, with the use of her walker, down the halls of E-wing, just as she always did, with only a slight alteration in her Wednesday routine. She was gliding down the hall to her turnaround destination located at Room 119, turned around, and made her way back, all the way back to her own room on the other end of the wing, passing by without stopping to talk to Old Man Perkinson. Gliding as though hovering slightly above the floor as she moved, gliding just as far and as long as she could go without exhausting herself. Gliding through life because what else does one do before the inevitable occurs?

———————◦———————

And so this went on. For Helen. For Mona. For Maisie. Was it for years? Or was it only days? Or merely for minutes? If for years, none of them ever seemed to get older.

If for only days, they all felt older by the minute.

6

Collapse

"PROMINENT LOCAL LAWYER KILLED IN HEAD-ON COLLISION." Even though the newspaper clipping was decades old and yellowed by time, the headline could still be easily read. It had remained painfully legible all these years; the piece of newspaper was held by magnets to the side of Helen McCardle's refrigerator. The headline was positioned next to the picture of a handsome young man, the same face as that of the handsome pale young man who sat in the next room. The pale man whom Helen often thought she could see through. The pale man whose only actions were to sit there and smile. The pale man who had lately begun to sneer at Helen. The pale man who created a greenish-gray glow that emanated from that room into the kitchen where Helen stood, trying to prepare lunch.

Helen felt especially fragile today. Her mind was cluttered with thoughts of despair and confusion. She had worked so hard for so long all by herself to keep the home in shape and solvent. And she was succeeding.

But he had sneered at her. He wasn't eating the meals she fixed, and she was wasting so much food. She had to eat by herself while he just sat there, watching television and occasionally smiling in her direction while she felt as though "that damn tube" was all that they shared anymore. All this she had gotten used to. Even the profound loneliness she often felt. But the sneers she could not handle. It was too much to bear. She was becoming unglued and cried more often. All her hard work paid for by a sneer.

Had she put the mustard on the sandwiches? Where was the mustard? It didn't matter. She would just take them in as is. She knew one would be wasted anyway, so what difference did it make? So she picked up the small tray she was using today, turned around, and froze in her tracks.

The handsome pale young man was glaring at her. His eyes had become wide with a menacing rage as his mouth slowly opened to reveal several layers of sharpened teeth. A loud guttural cackle came from deep inside him as first his mouth turned sideways and then his right eye started to slide in position down his formerly handsome face. As Helen watched in horror, his left eye migrated over to where his right eye had been so that his facial features had turned entirely sideways while his head remained in an upright position. His face then became as a spinning pinwheel, spinning faster and faster. Round and round. The tray had long dropped out of Helen's hands, its contents scattered and broken across the floor. Round and round his face spun until it stopped abruptly. And then his pale glowing head exploded.

Helen collapsed . . .

The quiet hum of machines, the echoes of muffled voices in the distance. It was a dimly-lit room with two beds, some rudimentary attempts at other furnishings such as a very small nightstand that doubled as a dresser and an oversized chair. People passed by the room, and occasionally, someone entered the room to check on its occupants.

When Helen awoke, or came to, or became alert, she was in this room—this hospital room. At her bedside, a full-figured woman with slightly curly, dark hair sat in the big oversized chair which she had pulled from its original place and positioned so that she could sit right by the bed. She had a hospital blanket draped around her shoulders to help keep her warm. She had been gently holding and caressing Helen's left hand, but when Helen's eyes opened, she got off of the chair and sat on the edge of Helen's bed and smiled.

"There you are, Mother," said Kathy tenderly. Helen blinked quietly and shook her head as if to jostle everything inside, so it would all return to its intended position. Helen's gaze settled on her daughter's face. "How are you feeling?" asked her daughter once Helen had a moment to compose her thoughts.

"I'm a little confused, Kathy," said Helen wearily, obviously still working on figuring out where she was and why she was there. "What happened?"

"Well you must've passed out and you fell. Hit your head pretty hard, Mother."

Helen reached up and patted at a bump on her forehead. She winced and laid her head back down onto the pillow. Mother and daughter sat there in silence for a while, giving Helen time to adjust to her surroundings. A tall slim young man walked into the room, pulling a computer station along with him.

"Good evening, Mrs. McCardle, I see you've woken up," he said.

He was a doctor who explained that he looked at all the X-rays and CAT scans and detected that everything was negative. There were no fractures, no broken hips, nor major head trauma. Her hypertension was back in check. Having kids who played in sports, Kathy made certain to ask if her mother had a concussion, and the doctor confirmed that, "No, just a nasty goose egg on her forehead." He then told them that it would be best if Helen stayed in the hospital overnight for observation, and she could go home first thing in the morning. Helen was especially relieved to hear that news.

She could go back home.

"Well, that's a relief, silly me. Guess I'm just too strong an old goat to let some blackout and tumble get me down for long," said Helen as if to dismiss the whole episode. She bent her head down and looked abashedly at her daughter before adding, "So I can get some rest tonight, go back home in the morning to your father, and everything will be back to normal. Just a little bump in the road of life." Helen nervously chuckled at the metaphor she had used and felt the painful bump on her forehead again.

"Mother, why don't you come spend some time with me and the kids?" offered Kathy as an alternative, trying to steer her mother's thoughts in a different direction.

"No, Kathy, I love you and Sam and the kids, but my place is at home with your father." Helen was quietly assertive despite her confusion, despite her obvious lack of grasp on reality.

Kathy was tired. It was a long day for her. She looked down and shook her head slightly before letting out a big, long tired sigh. It broke her heart to hear her mother talk like this. She loved her so much, was so proud of her mother's fierce and determined independence, but also realized that her mother was still not in her right mind . . . and she needed to take this opportunity to address the subject of her father. It was time. She needed to get this through to her mother, but it took a long time for her to speak.

"Daddy's . . . not home, Mother . . . he's . . . not there. You know that . . . don't you?" Kathy said haltingly as she kept a watchful eye on Helen, waiting to see how she would react, how she would "accept" this "news." Helen's reaction was both an expression of angry betrayal and confusion.

They were interrupted by a nurse who decided it was time to take Helen's vital signs and give her some medication the doctor who had just left the room a few minutes ago ordered. The nurse hung a new IV bag and jotted down a few notes to put on the computer as Kathy quietly talked to Helen while Helen sobbed slightly, holding her right hand to her mouth. Her hand was closed fist-like with her index finger resting on her upper lip and her thumb circling her lower lip; her torso rocked slightly forward and backward as she sat somewhat upright. Sometimes Helen nodded, and sometimes she shook her head, sometimes rubbing her index finger and thumb against each other as a way to help process and comprehend what she was hearing. Nothing her daughter said was what she wanted to hear, no matter how tenderly and gently Kathy brought her mother back to reality.

The nurse left the room as Helen just lay in the hospital bed looking at Kathy. She stayed silent, but her facial expression conveyed that she was finally grasping the reality of the situation.

"You do understand, don't you, Mother?" asked Kathy, searching her mother's face for comprehension and signs of clarity.

There was yet another long silence before Helen finally verbalized that she did indeed understand. However, it was palpable that Helen only partially accepted what Kathy had told her and that her plan to return home was undeterred. She was not going to recuperate from a silly fall in her daughter's home, even if her daughter used the word "recuperate" to mean addressing other issues.

"Okay. I give up on that idea. Mother, would you reconsider getting some help?" asked Kathy, slightly exasperated. She of course knew the answer to this question. But she asked it regardless as Kathy knew that her mother was still far more fragile than she was willing to admit and that in any condition, good or bad, she should have help anyway. So she didn't bother to wait for a response before asking another question. "Whatever happened to Spike?"

"Spike" was an African American home health nurse who had checked in on Helen on a regular basis in the past. Helen long ago abandoned calling this nurse her real name and simply called her Spike, partially because of her last name, Speicher, but mostly because she wore her hair in a very high bun with bursts of hair resembling spikes that rounded her head. Spikey spiked braids of hair that resembled a sunburst. The nurse so liked the nickname that Helen had given her that she actually used the moniker Spike more and more as time went on, often styling her hair in that signature pattern just to accentuate the association that had been created.

"Spike disappeared off the face of the earth," responded Helen curtly as if to convey that not only was Spike no longer making visits to her home but also attempting to close the entire subject on having any kind of outside help. What Helen specifically recalled but did not articulate to Kathy was a day not long ago when Spike stood at her door, with all her spikey spiked hair radiating in the sun, and Helen coldly turning her away saying she didn't need her services anymore. "And I *don't* need anybody else's help either," Helen added emphatically, just to make sure her point was made loud and clear.

"People don't just disappear from the face of the earth, Mother." Kathy's response was not scolding so much as it was incredulous at the obvious hyperbole in Helen's statement. "Or at least that you never hear about it in the news. So . . . what *really* happened? Did you tell her to stop coming? I know how bullheaded you are." Although their words were now a bit more pointed and direct than the soft loving tones made when Helen first awoke in her hospital bed, their discussion was not really heated or with direct anger. Kathy was merely a bit frustrated that her mother was too stubborn to accept help when help was readily available. "People don't just disappear from the face of the earth," she reiterated, adding, "and you DO need help!"

"I'm telling you, Spike disappeared off the face of the earth," Helen said this without a ring of falseness to her voice, regardless of whether she may or may not have told her to stop coming. "And I don't need help."

"Mother, you are crazy! You are literally going crazy!" The couplet blurted out of Kathy's mouth before she had a chance to stop herself. It's not what she wanted to say. It's not how she wanted to deal with her fragile mother. But she said it nonetheless, and the damage was done. Her mother would now stubbornly dig in her heels even firmer than she had, and nothing could be done until another accident occurred. And Kathy knew it would . . .

7

Spike

MONA STOOD ANXIOUSLY at the doorway. She alternately paced and stood still. Each alternate move served only to make her more anxious. Her husband Charles sat, watching television and occasionally peered over his big thick-rimmed black glasses in her direction. He was a bit more annoyed tonight than usual, knowing what night it was, and what ridiculous spectacle was about to take place.

He didn't even bother to look when he heard the door whisk open. He merely shook his head, knowing that Mona had just seen David arrive home and had dashed out to greet him. No, not greet him, ambush him was the correct term. For what Mona was doing to that poor young man was ambushing him. Sure enough, within minutes, the door opened again, and in walked Mona with David in tow.

"This will only take a minute, David. I'm so glad you were able to come over tonight." Mona's voice was breathless, nervous, and insincere all at once. "It's been so long . . . I . . . I mean *she* has missed you so much."

"MONA, STOP!" came the booming baritone voice from her husband as he rose out of his chair. For whatever reason, Charles' irritability had reached its boiling point, and his patience was at its limit. Mona was startled, taken aback by her husband's sudden outburst. She had already started to take David by the hand toward the stairway, but there was a large space between them, despite their connected hands because David was sort of frozen in place, not sure whose prompt to follow.

"David, I'm sorry about all of this. I really do appreciate your generosity of spirit in coming over here so often, but we really need to stop this. This is NOT helping anybody. I think you should just go on home," Charles was being truly apologetic to David, and the tone of his voice clearly conveyed this, but more than that, he wanted to finally take control of this ridiculous situation. He was also embarrassed that it was some other man who brought comfort to his wife instead of him. He felt many things, but mostly he felt it was time to stop this charade. If nothing else changed tonight, at least these visits from his well-meaning but far too obliging neighbor would end.

"Yes, uhh, Chuck, I don't want to cause any trouble," stammered the usually charming but utterly befuddled man who stood frozen with his hand still holding Mona's. He pulled it away and clasped his hands together and stood with his head bowed in a slightly penitent stance; if for no other reason than he felt so uncomfortable right now, he didn't know what other posture to assume. All natural ease and charm failed him in this instance.

For her part, Mona was stunned into silence. All she wanted was for David to go upstairs with her for a few moments, like always, and all would be right with the world again. But it was clear to her, given her husband's firm words, that this was not the time to voice any objections.

"Yes, uhh, I think I will just go home, Miss Mona. Maybe another night?" he said, gingerly trying to tread lightly between the two, realizing there was no easy way to escape this incredibly uncomfortable situation. He walked backward in awkward steps until he reached the door and quietly slipped outside.

"That was uncalled for, Charles," scolded Mona, using his proper name rather than Charlie, which she usually used in less frustrating circumstances. "You know how much David's visits mean to her. *Now what* am I going to tell her?" She looked at him as though she really wanted a response. Really wanted an answer. No answer came to her. He just walked back to his chair and sunk down into it, setting his big thick-rimmed black glasses on the stand beside him and rubbing his forehead. Either he had a headache or he was deep in thought about the situation or both. His booming baritone voice stayed silent.

And so Mona just stood there for a moment, plotting how to proceed. She reluctantly ascended the stairs by herself. She would have to figure out how to break the news that David would again not be over. She thought that these days without even a quick visit from David were always the hardest for her, "I mean for *her*" as if to differentiate which "her" it was most difficult for.

Mona walked up to the door and slowly opened it. She walked into the beam of the faint greenish-gray glow. Mona took a deep breath and sat on the foot end of the bed, silently covering her face to gather her thoughts. At last, she looked at her.

Curled up at the head end of the bed, with her knees bent up to her chin and her hands wrapped around her legs, her rich brown body turned like white in the faint glow of the darkened room. The faint greenish-gray glow in the room actually emanated from *her*. She wore her hair in a very high bun with bursts of hair resembling spikes that rounded her head. Spikey spiked braids of hair that resembled a sunburst. She looked at Mona without saying a word. She had been in the room for a while now, for how long; she did not recall since she had lost all sense of actual time and was too paralyzed to leave the comfort this room brought to her.

"My darling," for Mona always now called her "my darling," not her given name and certainly not that silly nickname she had acquired merely from the shape of her hairstyle. "I'm sorry, but David isn't coming over again today," said Mona, trying to tenderly deliver the disappointing news, but then deflected blame by adding, "your father won't allow it." But there was no response. The woman curled up at the head end of the bed, the woman with the very high bun with spikey spiked bursts of hair resembling a sunburst just stared at her.

"I think you're starting to regress, my darling. You had been making so much progress with David's visits . . . whether it was right or wrong to bring him here. I don't know. I was grasping at straws, thinking of ways to bring you out of your catatonic state. After you had that accident that caused the miscarriage, and after that asshole husband you hitched your wagon and stars to just up and left you, it seemed like the only thing that helped you was the sight of David. It seemed to brighten your day. I guess it's because he in a way resembled that . . . him. Now I realize it was the wrong way to treat your depression." Still no response. Mona struggled with more thoughts of what to say.

But all of these thoughts and words after all this time didn't seem to make sense anymore. The tender speech she just gave now sounded ludicrous. Like it was made up, like fiction, and like very bad clichéd fiction at that. The frustration welled up in Mona's mind, and she needed to extricate herself from that room. Extricate herself from this whole implausible scenario.

She ran out of the room, closed the door, and leaned against the wall. Her breathing was heavy. She was on the verge of hyperventilating. She couldn't do this anymore simply because she couldn't think of what to say next or what to plan next. In fact, this whole story didn't make any sense at all anymore—a scorned lover, a bad accident, silent isolation, the perfect yet unattainable hero—but this is the situation that she currently found herself in, and she couldn't think of how to change the story. She ran down the steps.

Charles stood at the bottom of the stairway. Mona stopped abruptly at the landing and looked at him, and at once it became clear to her.

"Jimmy, I can't do this anymore!" cried Mona . . . no, not Jimmy, "Chuck, I can't . . . " no, it was Charlie, that is what she called her loving husband. "Charlie, I can't do this anymore!" as she sunk into his big strong arms.

"I know you can't, my love" was all Charles could say as he embraced her gently. Her grasp on him was so tight, much more powerful a grasp than what a woman of her physique could normally muster. It was as though she was clinging to him for dear life. "We need to get you some help, Mona, more than I can give. You need professional help to sort out all these things . . ." he let her grasp him as hard as she needed to. ". . . these things in your mind," Charles added after giving her a chance to regain a little bit of composure.

"In your mind." The words hit Mona. The words were colder and clearer than ice. She was shakily ready to confront reality.

"She's . . . not there, is she?" admitted Mona as a few tears, stained black from eye makeup, ran down her cheeks. "She's not there." She sniffled a few times and left his embrace to find something to dab at her face. Charles took care of that for her, rubbing his shirtsleeves under her eyes. He pulled out his handkerchief to dab at her nose. "She's not there," she repeated, this time with an incredulous giggle.

"No, Mona, she's not there, and she hasn't been there for a long time," said Charles comfortingly, his otherwise booming baritone lowered to just above a whisper. His big thick-rimmed black glasses were marked with as many tears as Mona's face was. "You never really dealt with losing her, but I think now you're ready. I was wrong to go along with this for so long, pretending she was upstairs. It just seemed to make you happy, and I've so desperately wanted you to be happy again. But I realize I was wrong, and that's why I told David tonight that this has to stop. We needed a catalyst to set something off inside of you. It's time you got someone to help you through this. Real help. It's time."

She again clung to him, even tighter than a moment ago. Together they walked toward the door. She slowly put on a cape while Charles turned off the television, a few lights, and wiped off his big thick-rimmed black glasses. "Let's just go now, Mona. I will come back and pack a bag for you, but let's go now before we change our mind." His voice had returned to its natural booming baritone, but it was much subtler and far more comforting as he spoke. Together, arm in arm, they walked out of the door, not unlike the way they first stepped inside this door many years ago.

Mona looked at the woods that enveloped either side of their house; across the street, all was quiet and still. This silence and tranquility around them were a welcome respite from the intense sadness that had come to represent the inside of their home.

8

Helen, Content

AMAZINGLY, IT HAD taken just a few days to accomplish, but Helen's life was back to normal. The only reminder of that unfortunate incident was the presence of a bandage on her forehead. Actually, she was now better than she had been in a very long time. That one day and one night in the hospital rejuvenated her so much that her mind was clearer, her body was stronger, and she was more determined than ever to preserve life as she knew it. She had faced reality and clarity during that one twenty-four-hour period in the hospital. She now not only knew that where she wanted to be was at home, her precious home, but now she had the fortitude to make it be so.

It's true, "home" is only a material place in the sense of a dwelling, but the essence of home itself resonates in the soul; it creates that single spot in the entire universe where one feels as though the core of their being belongs *"there."* For many, the location of this essence can change periodically and effortlessly. But not for Helen. This home, physically and spiritually, is where she belonged. She and her husband personally designed and built it long ago, and she had put far too much of her soul into this place to just leave it, to sell it to some other people who could never understand and appreciate this one particular space in the world as she could.

She had eschewed staying with Kathy, Sam, and the kids in favor of putting her world back in order. Her strength, vitality, the lilt in her steps, and the smile on her face had proven she was right to make this decision.

Helen had mowed the lawn earlier today, and she was not tired. She cleaned most of the house today and replaced a rusty hinge on the screen door to the backyard and did not feel exhausted. She occasionally glanced over at that old yellowed newspaper clipping on the refrigerator and did not feel sadness or the need to shed a tear. The picture of that handsome young man, that headline, "PROMINENT LOCAL LAWYER KILLED IN HEAD-ON COLLISION," the story beneath it, none of these affected her today. For Helen was revitalized and content.

Having accomplished all that she had, it was time to make a slightly late lunch, sit down and relax, and simply cherish anew the life that she had carved for herself. So she stood at the kitchen counter, preparing sandwiches, like she often did for lunch, because sandwiches were easy. She was so full of energy and so clear of mind that she didn't even struggle to remember whether she had already put the mustard on the sandwiches. Her mind and body were clear of what had been ailing her, and it was such a liberating feeling. It was all a confirmation that she was right.

She occasionally looked to the adjoining room, to the handsome pale young man sitting on the chair. The man whom she sometimes thought she could see through. The cool greenish-gray glow that emanated from the room felt paradoxically like warmth to her. Yes, he still sat there silently, but he was smiling. He did not sneer at her like he had been doing recently. All smiles.

She practically waltzed as she carried the tray of sandwiches into the room; there was a flowing rhythm to her steps as she set up the tray tables and put the sandwiches on them. She gracefully threw herself upon the chair beside the handsome pale young man, and she sat there for a minute and took it all in and smiled.

"Your daughter tried to take you away from me," Helen said with only a small hint of bitterness in her voice. It was much more spoken as if it was a statement of self-appraising victory. Her words broke into the silence of the room, a space previously filled by only the very low volume of the television. "I couldn't let her do that. I know she cares. She thinks her heart is in the right place, but she doesn't understand. This is where you belong, this is where *we* belong, and I'm not crazy."

"She said that I was crazy. She actually said that to me in the hospital," she added, incredulous that her own daughter would've said that, would've implied such a thing.

The handsome pale young man just sat there glowing in his big comfortable chair, occasionally smiling back at her. But mostly, he just stared at the television.

Mostly, Helen stared through him.

But Helen didn't mind. She didn't mind that he simply just sat there. She didn't mind "that damn tube" as the one connection they seemed to have. She didn't mind eating her sandwich alone or that he didn't touch his at all. She didn't mind all the work that she had done today, or all the work she had yet to do. She didn't mind putting the tray tables away and discarding his uneaten food in the trash. She didn't mind the profound loneliness that had just now suddenly returned within the fraction of a second.

She didn't even mind that when all of this hard work and effort was done, the handsome pale young man with the warm greenish-gray glow sneered at her. He sneered at her. She didn't mind because at least his head didn't explode this time. For this was the life that she cherished.

Helen was content.

Helen was content?

9

The Crash

ON MAIN STREET, a few blocks from the county courthouse where she worked was a quaint little Italian restaurant nestled between a hardware store and an upscale men's clothier. A small alley, almost unnoticeable, was between the restaurant and the hardware store. At least once a month, she would set up a "girls' lunch" date with her best friend Wendy. Since they both had careers and families with kids involved in various after-school activities, they rarely had time to devote to their decades-long friendship. Having lunch at Rose Marie's with an old comrade on a regular basis was a must and would have to be enough, for now, for Helen's daughter, Kathy, to feel as though her life was about more than just career, family, and soccer games.

Kathy and Wendy had arrived with the first of the lunch crowd, and so were able to snag one of the coveted booths by the window. They ordered, sipped on water and coffee while waiting to eat and chatted.

"I see Austin and Alex won their last soccer match to get into district finals," said Wendy, for even though this was "their time," much like coworkers who socialize outside of work invariably discuss work, it couldn't be helped but to discuss their families.

"It's Xela now," said Kathy, rolling her eyes. "Alex has decided he wants to be referred to as 'Xela'. He's always been in Austin's shadow, so now he's focusing more on art and feels Xela is the kind of name an artist would have. He won't admit it, but it's because he doesn't like being compared to his older brother so much, so this is his way of becoming his own person. Sam and I are just going with it. But yes, they won their match which means even more road trips for a few more weeks." Kathy let out a big puff of air and rolled her eyes again. Despite her body language, she was very proud of her boys' accomplishments.

"I gotta tell ya, It just doesn't end, does it?" laughed Wendy. "I'm dealing with field hockey and cheer tournaments this weekend *and* next."

"Not for two more years, and then who knows what I'll have to deal with once they go to college."

Outside on the street, there was the sudden loud sound of tires screeching to a halt on the pavement followed by several car horns. The noise was so violently loud that it alarmed everyone in the restaurant. From their vantage point in the window booth, it appeared to Kathy and Wendy as though a car had exited the small alley from the direction of the hardware store parking lot and had pulled into the path of a car that had probably been driving too fast down Main Street. Since the car driving on the street had swerved slightly to the left to avoid a collision, a third car, traveling from the opposite direction, had also veered and come to a sudden stop. None of the cars had collided, and so after more loud noises in the form of more honking horns, the drivers all righted the direction of their vehicles and drove off.

But inside the restaurant, Kathy was frozen with her hand on her chest. Other than some movement from breathing, she seemed to be paralyzed for the few seconds it took her to compose herself. Seconds that felt like hours. "God" was all she could say.

Wendy looked at her old friend, waiting for her to work through the moment, which happened simultaneously with the arrival of their lunch. After the waiter placed the plates down and made a comment about the brief excitement outside, they began to eat.

"I swear, every time I hear something like that, it just . . ." Kathy broke off while twirling her fork in her food.

"It reminds you of your father's accident, doesn't it? I gotta tell ya, that was such an awful tragedy, and for you to have seen it . . ." Wendy knew all too well what Kathy was referring to and was switching into an acknowledging and comforting friend mode.

"That sound, that horrible screeching sound, it never leaves you," Kathy said, shaking her head and working on putting her mind back on lunch. "You'd think after all these years that sound wouldn't affect me, but it's the most horrible sound in the world to me."

They started to eat, but it was now clear that girls' lunch for today was not going to be the lighthearted fun escape that it usually is. Reawakened hurt and lingering wounds from tragedies, even long ago ones, do not just disappear instantly once they resurface.

"So how is your mother doing?" asked Wendy, changing the subject but not by too much. She knew of last week's fall and brief hospital stay.

"Oh, she's back at home. Doing everything. Acting like everything is fine. Stubborn. The usual," said Kathy, shaking her head.

"I gotta tell ya, your mother is such an inspiration, Kathy. To have faced all she has in life and . . ."

Kathy cut her off. "She *used* to be, Wendy. She used to be an inspiration. But I swear she's losing her mind. I do regret calling her crazy in the hospital, that didn't help matters any. But the things she says and does. Wendy, she is wasting so much food! And she's not as strong as she wants people to think she is. She can't really do what she used to do, and I just don't know what to do with her anymore. Regardless, I might not have to worry about making any decisions anyway."

"What do you mean by that?" Wendy said in response to that last puzzling statement.

"After she was in the hospital last week, someone from the Area Agency on Aging contacted me. We had a long talk. They're concerned about her abilities . . . and her mental status." Kathy gave Wendy a more detailed account of what had transpired during the past week. "I don't know what's going to happen, but I don't think she will like it."

"Yikes, Kathy, that sounds serious. I didn't realize it was that bad. But I gotta tell ya, as long as it's someone else stepping in, she can't put the blame on you. And let's face it, they can help her. I mean, really, really help her."

The two finished their meals and went back to work, vowing to have another girls' lunch much sooner than they normally would since this one had gotten sidetracked with the memories of grief and sadness and the long conversation about Helen.

Elsewhere in town on E-wing at the facility, it was anything but grief and sadness today. It was a day full of hope and the chance for renewal; time to put grief and sadness in the past. Maisie Dearborn was gliding down the hall, past the nurses' desk full of bustling working nurses and the other staff. She was on her daily journey to the far end of the wing, near the big picture window, near the exit door. As she approached her usual turnaround point, Room 119, she stopped as always. She gazed at the door as always and at the paintings around it as always. But today, she did not turn around after her brief rest. Today, she had a reason not to.

Today, she had a reason to enter 119, not just use it as her turning point. And so Miss Maisie opened the door to walk in.

"Mother?" whispered a faint, weary voice from inside the room.

10

Reunion

MAISIE HAD OPENED the door of 119 by maneuvering her walker so that she could use it to help push the door open. Little by little, she'd push on the big heavy door then push the walker up against it, take a step, and then repeat the action until she was entirely inside the room. Once inside, and with the door pushed slightly closed, Maisie ditched her walker and made a few halting steps toward the hospital bed in the room.

"Mother, use your walker. You know you can't take a step without it".

"Oh, I *can*," said Maisie. "I can take a few steps just fine. I just have to go slowly and balance myself that's all. Its good exercise," she chuckled.

Mona had been lying flat on her left side in the bed but adjusted herself to more of a sitting position now that Maisie had come in to visit. Her hair was let down past her shoulders; she looked tired, frail, and empty. She didn't have enough time to gather her thoughts and physical abilities to offer much assistance as Maisie found her way to the bed and sat on the foot end.

"Besides, having you here has given me an extra spring in my step. I waited so long to see you again. I just didn't know it would be like this." Again, Maisie chuckled, just a little chuckle as she was trying to make sure that Mona knew she was happy to see her and not angry that she had avoided visiting in such a long time.

"I know. I'm sorry about that, Mother. You know I've not been well myself."

"I know dear," and with this, Maisie got up and worked her way to the head end of the bed and gave Mona a motherly hug and a tender kiss on her forehead. After a long quiet embrace, Maisie returned to sitting near the end of the bed

"I've practically not left the house in . . ."

"Agoraphobia," Maisie interrupted.

"I don't have agoraphobia, Mother. I've been trying to deal with . . ." Mona did not finish her sentence yet although soon she would need to get the courage to do so.

"Imagine you ending up here," said Maisie, once she was sure that Mona had trailed off and wasn't going to finish her thought. She looked around the dimly-lit room, sparsely decorated since it had been vacant with no full-time tenant, "here in this room, why I walk past this room every single day," she observed.

"It's only for a few days until they find a more suitable room for me in the main hospital. The loony bin was full . . . full of other crazy people." The last words sounded so harsh. "There's a lot more out there, like me, who lost focus on how to cope with their lives, their losses, and their pain. Not just me," Mona added the last part defensively. When her husband Charles initially brought her to the hospital, the admissions clerk had said the psychiatric ward was full but that they would find a room somewhere in the facility for her. It was Charles who suggested E-wing, which was near the ward if there was an open room. He suggested it partially in the hope that Mona could spend some time with Maisie while she was being evaluated for admission and therapy. Since Mona had posed no threat to herself or anyone else, the facility was able to accommodate this suggestion. She added, "But I'm happy to see you again, Mother, and I'm truly sorry I stayed away for so long. Surely you can't be mad at me for going crazy."

"You're not crazy, my dear, you just need to face your grief. It's kept you paralyzed. It's finally time to move on and embrace life again," said Maisie in comforting pep talk tones.

"Embrace life? My daughter WAS my life, and now she's dead! And the rest of the world just keeps on going on . . . like nothing happened. People come and go, they leave for work, they leave for vacation, they come home and take out the trash. They do the most mundane things and act as though living is okay while my daughter is dead! Even Jimmy . . . I mean Charlie. He just goes on with life as if going on with life is OKAYYY," Mona said all these things as if she was carelessly rummaging through a box of clothes and just pulling out this piece and that piece and just slinging them around the room. It didn't matter where they landed, where the words went, where the clothes landed. They just need to get out of that box, out of her head. She was trapped in a tangled jumble of the stages of grief that she could not, would not, process.

"Charles feels pain, my dear, and he still feels it from time to time, but he dealt with 'going on' a long time ago," said Maisie, clarifying that pain never really goes away; it is just dealt with when it rears its mournful head.

"You don't know what it's like to lose a child," Mona said bitterly, feeling as though her mother was discounting her stultified grief and temporarily oblivious to the fact that Maisie also had to deal with the death of Mona's daughter . . . the death of Maisie's granddaughter.

Maisie just sat there. She was not a counselor with the perfect words to say that guide a person toward self-realization or healing. She was a mother, acting on instincts and dealing with her own sense of grief and loss experienced during her long lifetime. Dealing with the loneliness and abandonment she had lived with for so many years on E-wing, with no visits from a daughter she raised and loved so much, and on whom she had spent so much time rationalizing her absence. Maisie, too frail to live on her own and yet too strong to die, living a life where the rituals of daily existence were her only comfort. But those particular words stung more than a thousand lonely days– "you don't know what it's like to lose a child."

To her daughter, Maisie said, "I feel like I lost you a long time ago . . ."

11

Helen's Decision

THE SANDS OF time had shifted to a new standstill. Maisie now spent all of her so-called recreational time in Room 119, neglecting all other friendships and all other interests. Maisie relished this period of time–the return of a prodigal child and the healing of their relationship.

Again, the days felt like weeks, and the weeks felt like minutes. If time and change had come to that kind of standstill during those days for Maisie, at the far end of the outskirts of town, the winds of both were about to destroy the façade of a woman who had spent so many years fiercely fighting the very thought of them existing.

This morning left Helen feeling nervous and tense. She sat in the kitchen, sometimes staring into the adjacent room, looking for the comforting greenish-gray glow that she had grown accustomed to, but mostly these days there was no such specter. Were these moments of clarity or were they signs that she was crazy after all? It had been like this ever since she returned from that night spent in the hospital. She had had that one utterly blissful day of serenity with the handsome pale young man in the other room, but since then, the sneers returned, and she found herself stumbling at times although always careful not to fall again. As she sat there, the formerly comforting glow flickered on and off. Formerly comforting. And mostly it was not there anymore.

The bigger cause for apprehension was that Kathy would be arriving in just a few minutes, but she wouldn't be alone. Helen didn't want to think about what this meant, but she knew Kathy was upset that Helen had undone all the work that Kathy did two weeks ago when she had fallen and spent that day and night in the hospital when Helen refused all forms of help and insisted that she was okay. Now fear was growing inside Helen, and she was becoming too exhausted to fight.

Despite knowing that Kathy would arrive with "some representative," Helen nevertheless felt betrayed when she opened the door because not only was this strange man standing there with Kathy but there were also two gentlemen in white uniforms, waiting just beyond the front stoop. The patches on their uniforms matched the insignia on the side of a van parked near where they stood.

Helen composed herself and opened the door slowly, offering a nervously clipped greeting to her daughter. "Mother, this is David Blank, the guy I talked to you about yesterday," said Kathy as she and David walked inside the house. Helen turned away briefly but spun around just as quickly to prove that she was composed and motioned for them to sit down. Only David sat down because Kathy had slipped into the other room.

"Hi, Mrs. McCardle, I'm David Blank. I'm the director of the facility your daughter has talked to you about, and I would like to sit down and tell you about all the programs and living options and housing arrangements we have to offer to help you". David, in this instance, was being far more professional than his usual charming, yet still professional self, but it would not have made a difference; no amount of charm would work here. No wink, no calming words, or handsomely-chiseled face could win over this woman in this situation; it had to be strictly business and straightforward.

"Okay then, I understand. We can talk about what you have to offer. Have a seat. Would you like some coffee? Kathy, can you . . ." Helen actually hadn't noticed that Kathy had stepped into the other room; only that when Kathy returned, the room remained as still as it had been, no comforting glow emanated from there. The three of them sat down to go over the proposals regarding what David had come to discuss with Helen, hoping to convince her to make a decision, one that he and Kathy had predetermined her to make.

During the brief presentation in the kitchen, if it could be called a presentation since it felt more like an ambush, Helen could see outside. She could see the two men standing out there. They both had cell phones and had been using them, either playing games or texting or whatever, and one of Helen's neighbors had walked over, and they were talking to him. She could see the neighbor shaking his head and making swirling motions with the fingers of his one hand while motioning toward her yard with his other hand. It looked like he was telling them how crazy she is. It all felt like such an invasion, a calculatedly calm invasion full of betrayal, and everyone, even the neighbors, were in on it. Helen calmly but firmly slapped both palms on the table as she stood up; no need to make a scene to prove them all correct.

"I'm sorry, Mr. Blank, but I don't need the services of your facility. I am quite fine here at home, and I can manage everything . . . just like I've been doing for all these years. It was very nice of you to discuss all of this with me, and I'm sorry to have wasted your time, but my answer is no."

It felt so easy, so reaffirming for Helen to so politely and rationally decline David's offer that she no longer needed to tower over him from her position of power and sat back down.

David looked over at Kathy, giving a shrug and lifted his hands in an "I tried" gesture. Kathy knew what this meant, and it was her turn to try to talk to her mother.

"Mother . . ." Kathy started very firmly. "Mother, you have fallen four times in the last year, and you've been hospitalized twice for exhaustion. It's a miracle you haven't broken a hip or worse. Your mind is not as clear as it used to be. You just can't do this anymore! Why don't you listen to reason?"

"Kathy, I'm fine. Those falls were just a couple clumsy episodes. I'm more careful now. The doctor said I am very healthy. I *want* to stay here. I love this house, this is my home. My *home,* Kathy, for forty years. I've got my strength back, and my mind *IS* clear. I don't ask you or Sam or the kids for much help. Really, I don't ask for anything. I do it all. I know you all seem to think I'm crazy, but it's my life . . . and my decision." Helen was resolute; sure she had convinced both visitors that she was sane, healthy, and perfectly capable.

If that felt effortless, what came next would shatter Helen's reserve completely.

"Mommm. . ." Kathy sat down; she looked over at David, who had some papers in his hand. He purposely shifted them ominously as he looked at Kathy. His clear intention was to have Kathy continue to persuade her mother to change her mind. "Mother, this isn't just about 'you'," Kathy said as a few tears welled up in her eyes, preparing for what she had to say. She knew this would hurt worse than anything else since her father's accident.

"It's no longer really your choice, Mother. The county is stepping in," Kathy said slowly, gingerly.

"The Area Agency on Aging is looking at this as a possible case of elder abuse," David added as Kathy winced. She had hoped this particular bit of information would not need to be revealed to her mother.

But the damage was done.

"ELDER ABUSE? . . . ABUSE?" Helen let out a viscerally primal scream and bolted out of her chair, darting backward as though the table was on fire, rapidly shaking her head in small very quick vibrations. She couldn't believe the words she had just heard. "No." She refused to give any kind of credence to the words this complete stranger just said. She looked at David, unsure whether he was an authority regarding these possible allegations or what role he had in this, beyond what he had discussed about the facility only minutes before. David made a very slight nod, confirming that his words were accurate; he looked away for just a moment, himself a bit overwhelmed by Helen's visceral reaction.

"Mrs. McCardle, we have a case of a very sick elderly person who's in an environment where proper care is not being given," David said emphatically.

Helen stood frozen looking into the other room, and for one last brief glorious moment, the comforting greenish-gray glow returned. She lifted her head as tears streamed down her face to bask in its comforting warmth . . . for it was comforting warmth to her. The source of that glow, the handsome pale young man sat in there, giving her one last smile before he and that glow that emanated from him disappeared completely and permanently.

Though tears continued flowing down her face, that brief visage brought an ephemeral smile to her face. Forty years of memories flooded Helen's mind. She darted to the refrigerator and pushed away the magnets that held the faded old newspaper clipping to the side of it and pulled the paper off, partially ripping off an edge that had fused to the appliance. She looked at it and held it out so that both Kathy and David could see the handsome face near the headline "PROMINENT LOCAL LAWYER KILLED IN HEAD-ON COLLISION."

"I know that to you, all you see is an elderly man that can't walk or talk or even eat, who just lies in a bed set up in a living room, but to me, I see this. Every time I go in that room, when I am with him, this is what I see: I see the man I fell in love with, the man I've loved for almost fifty years, the man I have taken care of, bathed, fed, clothed, day in and day out ever since he was in that accident. I don't see an elderly old cripple like you do, I see this . . . this handsome man I love. I have dedicated my life to being here for him, and I have done everything I can for us to keep our home, to be together, to stay together for the rest of our lives like the vows we took on our wedding day. And you call this abuse? *Abuse*?"

Though tears were still streaming down Helen's face as she gestured toward her husband lying in the bed in the living room, Kathy stopped crying and had managed to compose herself. "No one is saying you abuse daddy, Momma, what we're saying is you can no longer take care of him properly on your own. You're not being realistic if you think you can take all of this on by yourself. You refuse to accept any kind of help, you've turned away every home care attendant for months . . . for no reason at all . . . even Spike who daddy really seemed to respond to."

"I can confirm Ms. Speicher had reported that you told her to stop checking in," David added, having seen that report from Helen's former home health nurse.

"I told Spike to stop coming by because she kept trying to get me to put him in a nursing home, just like you two are now. And that is something I vowed I would never do. I want to take care of him here at home. *Our* home," Helen said defiantly.

David felt the need to interject regarding her husband's condition and well-being. "Well, the last time you were in the hospital and your husband had to be put in temporary care, the nursing staff took notice of some bedsores, which are a serious threat to his health given his fragile state."

"Momma, they're not getting any better. I just checked them. Momma, please. When you fell two weeks ago and had to stay in the hospital overnight, I worked my ass off making arrangements for care for daddy, and then they discovered the bedsores, and *he* had to be hospitalized too, only to have you undo everything and bring him back home instead of keeping him in extended care. I was so furious with you, Mother. Everyone knows you have done a great job taking care of daddy all these years, but he wasn't always completely bedridden like he is now. Ever since he had to have that feeding tube placed, his condition has gotten worse. He really needs the kind of help like the facility this man is offering you. *You* need it too. They can manage his feeding tube a lot better than you can," Kathy said.

"On his last admission, he was determined to be slightly malnourished," David concurred.

"That damn tube," Helen allowed herself to laugh, to finally laugh at all of this, and to start to feel a sense of clarity regarding what she had been putting herself through all this time. "Oh, Kathy, if only you knew how many times I've fumbled and struggled with trying to feed him and said 'that damn tube'. Sometimes it feels like that's all we share together any more. He just lays there. I can't do it, Kathy, I just can't do it." Helen was also finally admitting that this was all too much for her to handle.

"Our facility," David said, seeing his chance, "has some wonderful little stand-alone cottages and some are available right now! Today. You will have someone come in every day and help you with taking care of your husband. You can both live there together. It will be like your own home."

"Mother, you just can't handle this property any longer. The yard work alone is killing you. You've worked so hard for so many years and look what it's doing to you . . . and you are just too damn stubborn to accept help. I know you love this house. I *grew up* in this house. I love it too, but it's just too much. And it's too far away from town for the kind of help you need. Now that daddy needs a different kind of care . . ."

"That's where we can help you, Mrs. McCardle," David said.

"You're not a failure, Mother. Everyone admires what you have done, and how you've been dedicated to daddy all these years when someone else would've just put him away and gone on and lived a life free of all this responsibility. You have no idea how proud I am of you for standing by daddy all this time when he's been practically unable to give anything back to you for years."

"I love your father, Kathy, and I'm entirely devoted to him . . . in sickness and in health," Helen's voice was tender, her face expressing the essence of utter and complete love. "No accident could ever change that. But you're right . . . I guess as long as we're together, it doesn't matter where we are. It's not this house. It's not this piece of land. It is us being together that makes a home."

The two men who had been waiting by the van outside came in and transferred Helen's husband to a portable gurney and prepared to take him to the facility on the other side of town. David left separately after discussing a few details with Helen. Kathy needed to get to work, having already arranged to go in slightly late today, but reassured her mother that they didn't have to make any other decisions today, decisions about what to do with the house.

After gently caressing her husband's hair, kissing him on the forehead, and reassuring the motionless man she would be there by his side soon, Helen opted to stay at home to grab a few things and drive separately.

She stood alone in her kitchen. She stared at the barren space on the refrigerator where the old newspaper clipping had been for so many years before she tore it down this morning. That clipping that recounted the story of the horrible accident that claimed the life of her husband's law firm partner now lay on the table, unfolded, showing the pictures of both her husband and his deceased partner. Part of the body of the article was now torn off, still fused to the side of the refrigerator. Why the clipping had been mounted on the side of the appliance at all was now something she couldn't even explain. Who *can* explain how and why material objects such as that clipping affect our daily routines and rituals?

Helen made a sandwich. A single sandwich, not two, and went into the other room to sit down where she always sat. The sandwich sat on a single tray table she had pulled from out of the broom closet. She looked over at the chair, where the handsome pale young man usually "sat," and then past it to the bed in the room, where her husband usually lay. The chair was now permanently empty and so was the bed. She looked at the wide archway between the kitchen and this room, widened during a remodeling years ago to accommodate more space for that very hospital bed that was now empty. She looked at the blank television screen. The house felt so empty. It felt so cold and uncomforting. This had been their home for forty years, but without him there, it meant nothing; it was merely a piece of space on earth. Despite many years of mostly silence from the man she loved, the house now felt more deafeningly quiet than at any time before.

She sat there for what seemed like an unbearable eternity. Every second of that eternity robbed her of precious time she could instead spend with the love of her life.

Helen stood up; she would leave now to join him at the facility. She could come back later today to get some things. Still later, she would decide what to do with the house and with everything in it. But those decisions would come easier now that it certainly did not feel like home anymore.

She walked into the kitchen with her untouched sandwich on the plate, and for the last time in her life, Helen threw one uneaten sandwich into the garbage can.

12

Coda/The Housekeeper

IT FELT LIKE a fresh beginning. It was a new day; the morning was already sunny with a nice summer breeze. David Blank backed his car out of his garage and backed slowly down the driveway. Already, his new position had brought vindication that he made the right career move, having successfully helped an older couple in dire need of direction and help. He backed out onto Woods Drive, admiring the long line of untouched nature that ran across the street from his and his neighbor's homes. For as far as the eyes could see, nothing but pristine woods, fields, and wildflowers. Maybe it was selfish for his neighborhood association to fight so hard to keep one entire side of the road undeveloped, but the town in which he lived badly needed at least one area not corrupted by man. And so David drove past that long stretch of woods toward work, ready to embrace another day in his new position at the facility.

At the facility, Miss Maisie was also ready to embrace another day. One that would be spent in Room 119, working on catching up on so many lost years. As she glided toward the nurses' desk, heading from one end of the long corridor toward the other end, she passed by a room with a new arrival. In it were Helen and her husband, who were there temporarily to treat his bedsores and malnutrition before heading to live in one of the cottages that were outside at the other end of the corridor, just outside the big picture window that Maisie walked to each day.

Simone Speicher had been sitting at a computer going over some forms at the nurses' desk but needed to get up to take care of some business. "Hey, Victoria, I'm going to go look in on the McCardles. I'm going to show Mrs. McCardle one of the cottages available and see how she's handling all this. It's been a while since I've seen her and her husband." She grabbed her long braids, and in one effortless swoop, she clipped them up into a high bun on her head, forming spikes that rounded her head. Spikey spiked braids of hair that resembled a sunburst.

Simone's path crossed with Maisie as she walked in the direction of the McCardles' room. "Hi, Miss Maisie, don't run over me now," said she, faking a dodge-out-of-her-way move as Maisie waved and chuckled and glided toward her destination. Maisie could hear Simone say, "I'm so excited to see you here . . ." and a warm return greeting of "Hi, Spike,

I'm sorry about the whole . . ." before gliding out of hearing distance of that room.

Dr. Ekema Olinga got up from the computer chart he had been studying at the nurses' station and ran one of his hands across the top of his slightly graying, shortly cropped hair. When he turned around, he saw Maisie through his big thick-rimmed black glasses and walked over toward her as she was passing by. His dark-skinned big muscular frame towered over the little old lady as she stopped for a moment. In a booming baritone voice, Dr. Olinga told Maisie that he was just checking her records and that everything looked great.

"All your exercising is actually making you younger, dear girl. Keep up the good work," he said encouragingly with both pride for successful treatment of one of his favorite patients and genuine glee for her improved health.

"Oh, I imagine it has helped me a little, that and other things . . . and I will!" responded Maisie with a little chuckle. "Thank you, doctor," added Maisie as she continued on her way down the long E-wing corridor, and Dr. Olinga walked off in another direction toward another wing in the facility.

Maisie continued her journey of gliding with her walker toward the other end of E-wing as she always had. She stopped at Room 119 to stare at the door for just a moment before going in. She was so excited to spend yet another day reconnecting with Mona, for as long as Mona would be in the unit, this would be her new mission in life.

So singularly focused and dedicated was she that she didn't realize that she wasn't alone as she stood outside the door of Room 119. As she put her frail old hand on the door handle, she was startled when she heard a voice in the hall call out to her from behind.

"Miss Maisie, darling. What are you doing?" It was Reva, the plump little housekeeper. She had been pushing her cleaning cart closely behind Maisie and her walker down the length of the corridor, but of course she wasn't moving as smoothly and swiftly as Maisie was. No one did.

Maisie looked almost guilty as she stared speechlessly at Reva. She took her hand off the door handle and used her walker to move backward just a few steps. She chuckled and at last said, "Oh, nothing, this is where I stop every day before I turn around and go back to my room," and she chuckled again, a bit nervously, having been caught off guard.

Reva pushed her cleaning cart aside and smiled at Maisie as she went about her business. She walked up to the door of 119, pushed it open a crack, and stepped inside just a foot or two, reached for two bottles of bathroom cleaner off the first shelf and pulled down a dust-collecting sweeping cloth from the next shelf up. She then grabbed a handful of rolls of bathroom tissue and used all these items to restock her cart.

"You wanna help me do some of my cleaning today, Miss Maisie?" Reva inquired since Maisie was still standing there, nearly frozen, watching Reva.

"Child, you can do the whole thing today if you want, I am tiiired!" said Reva, emphasizing and elongating the word tired.

"No. no. I never was one to do a lot of housework," again Maisie chuckled nervously and started to turn around to glide back down the hall in the direction of her room at the other end of the wing. "I'm getting a little tired myself," she said.

On her way back to her room, she sat down beside Old Man Perkinson, something she hadn't been doing lately. He welcomed her in his usual grouchy manner, perhaps even grouchier because he made sure to point out that she had been ignoring him for days.

"Arthur, calm down. You're going to set your pacemaker off again," said Maisie. She quickly and effortlessly eased back into the bickering banter she shared with her dear old friend.

They would do this daily for many days to come.

It was comforting to return to her normal routine and put the ghosts of yearning back away.

Made in the USA
Middletown, DE
08 December 2017